# The Little Match Girl

Hans Christian Andersen

# THE
# Little
# Match Girl

*illustrated by*
Blair Lent

*Houghton Mifflin Company, Boston*

IT WAS dreadfully cold. The snow was falling and it was almost dark on the last evening of the old year.

In the cold and gloom a poor little girl was wandering through the streets. She carried a number of matches in an old apron and she held a bundle of them in her hand. No one had bought any matches from her all day long, and no one had given her so much as a single penny.

When she had left home she had been wearing slippers, but they had been of little use. They were very big slippers; much too big, for they had belonged to her mother. The little child had lost them as she was running across the road to get out of the way of the carriages that went racing by.

One slipper was not to be found again. The other had been picked up by a boy who had run off with it, thinking he could use it as a doll's cradle someday when he had children of his own. So the little girl walked on, her bare feet almost frozen with the cold.

Shivering with cold and hunger she crept along. She looked a picture of misery. Poor little girl! The snowflakes were falling on her long fair hair, which hung in pretty curls over her neck; but she did not think of that now. Lights were shining in the windows, and there was a glorious smell of roast goose in the air, for it was New Year's Eve. Yes, she did think of that!

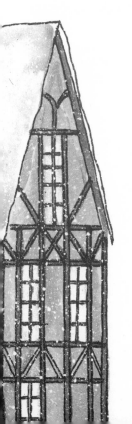

The little girl found a corner where one house projected a little beyond another and she crouched there, drawing her little feet close under her. But she was still cold. She did not dare go home, for she had sold no matches, nor earned even one penny. If she should return home her father would surely give her a beating. And besides it was almost as cold at home as it was here, for they had nothing over them but a roof through which the wind whistled, even though the largest cracks had been stuffed with straw and rags.

Her little hands were almost numb with the cold. Ah! A match might warm them. If she could only take one from a bundle, and strike it against the wall. She took one out. R-r-atch! How it sputtered. How it burned! It was a warm bright flame, just like a tiny candle, and she held her hands around it. It was a wonderful little light, but it seemed very strange to her.

It suddenly seemed to the little girl as though she were sitting in front of a great polished stove that had bright brass feet and a brass cover. There was a fire blazing inside and it warmed her. How the fire burned! How comfortable it was!

But just as she was stretching out her feet to warm them the fire went out, the stove vanished, and she had only the remains of the burned match in her hand.

She struck another match against the wall. It blazed brightly and when the light fell upon the wall it became transparent like a thin veil, and she could see through it into a room. A table was spread with a snow-like cloth and set with a shining dinner service. A roast goose, stuffed with apples and dried plums, smoked gloriously.

And what was still more splendid to behold, the goose hopped down from the dish and waddled along the floor, with a knife and fork in its breast, right up to the little girl. And then . . .

The match went out, and only the thick, damp, cold wall was before her.

Again, she lighted another match—the flame shot up—and this time she was beneath a beautiful Christmas tree; it was greater and more ornamented than the one she had seen through the glass door at the rich merchant's house on Christmas day. Hundreds of candles burned upon the green branches, and tiny painted figures, like those she had seen in the shop windows, looked down upon her. The little girl reached out for them: then the match went out.

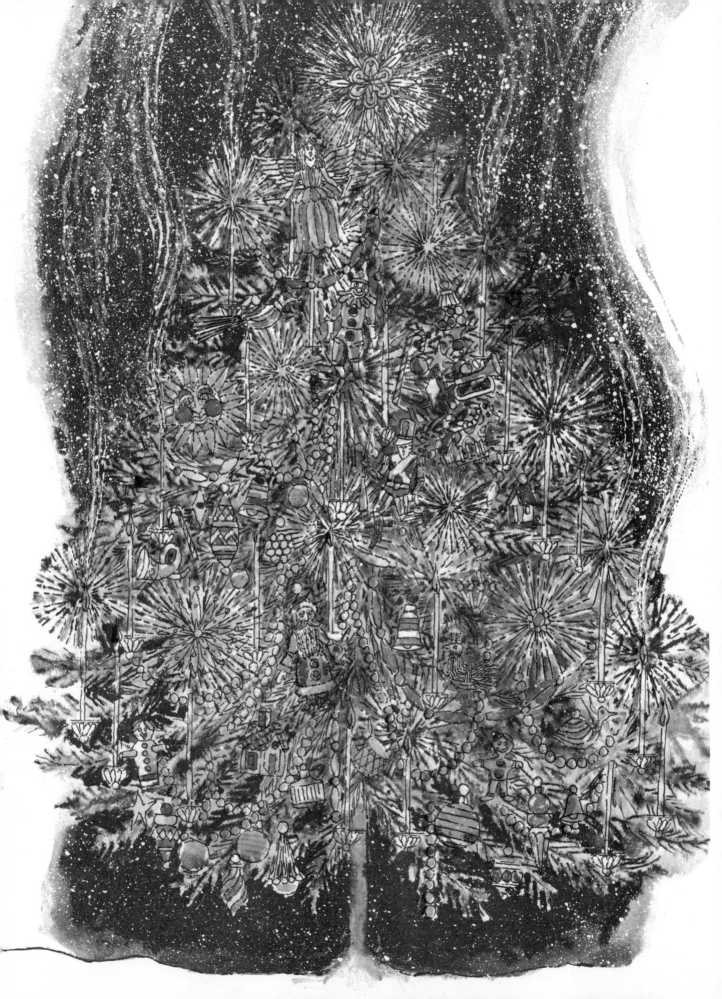

The Christmas lights burned brighter and then rose higher and higher until they became twinkling stars. One of them fell down and made a bright streak of light across the sky.

"Now someone is dying," thought the little girl. Her old grandmother, the only person who had loved her, and who was now dead, had told her that when a star fell down a soul rose up to heaven.

She rubbed another match against the wall; it became bright again, and in the glow her old grandmother stood clear and shining, kind and lovely.

"Grandmother!" cried the child. "Oh, take me with you! I know you will vanish when the match is burned out. You will vanish like the warm stove, the wonderful roast goose and the great glorious Christmas tree!"

She hastily struck a whole bundle of matches, for she wished to keep her grandmother with her. The matches burned with such a glow that it became brighter than the middle of the day. Her grandmother had never seemed so tall or so beautiful.

The grandmother took the little girl in her arms, and they both soared in brightness and joy above the earth, very, very high; up to where neither cold, nor hunger, nor fear is ever known.

In the cold morning light the poor little girl was
found crouched in the corner by the wall; her cheeks
were glowing, her lips smiling, but she had been
frozen to death on the last night of the old year. The
New Year's sun shone upon the lifeless child as she
sat there with the matches on the snow. One bundle
of them was all burned out.

"She had wanted to warm herself," the people said. But no one imagined what beautiful things she had seen, or with what joy and gladness the little girl and her grandmother had gone into the New Year.

The End